EASTER

POEMS

EASTER
POEMS

selected by
Myra Cohn Livingston

illustrated by
John Wallner

Holiday House
New York

TO NORMA FARBER

1909–1984

Text copyright © 1985 by Myra Cohn Livingston
Illustrations copyright © 1985 by John C. Wallner
Printed in the United States of America
First Edition

Library of Congress Cataloging in Publication Data
Main entry under title:

Easter Poems.

   Summary: A collection of poems on Easter themes by
John Ciardi, William Jay Smith, Joan Aiken, and other
authors, including poems translated from Russian
and German.
   1. Easter—Juvenile poetry.   2. Children's poetry.
[1. Easter—Poetry.   2. Poetry—Collections]
I. Livingston, Myra Cohn.   II. Wallner, John C., ill.
PN6110.E2E255   1985   808.8'1933   84-15866
ISBN 0-8234-0546-X

CONTENTS

EASTER

On Easter morn
Up the faint cloudy sky
I hear the Easter bell,
   Ding dong . . . ding dong . . .
Easter morning scatters lilies
On every doorstep;
Easter morning says a glad thing
Over and over.
Poor people, beggars, old women
Are hearing the Easter bell . . .
   Ding dong . . . ding dong . . .

      HILDA CONKLING

LITTLE CATKINS

Little boys and little maidens
Little candles, little catkins
     Homeward bring.

Little lights are burning softly,
People cross themselves in passing—
     Scent of spring.

Little wind so bold and merry,
Little raindrops, don't extinguish
     These flames, pray!

I will rise tomorrow, early,
Rise to greet you, Willow Sunday,
     Holy day.

ALEXANDER BLOK
translated from the Russian
by Babette Deutsch

RABBITS ARE NICE NEIGHBORS

Rabbits are nice neighbors,
Kindly and quiet.
They don't bite mailmen,
Or make loud noises in the night.

Rabbits are ornamental,
Lop-eared and silky,
With long bouncy legs,
And noses that quiver.

And now and then—not often—
They deliver—
Eggs.

ZILPHA KEATLEY SNYDER

EASTER HABITS

Around now,
they think of rabbits.
(I don't know why.)

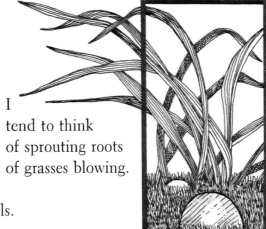

I
tend to think
of sprouting roots
of grasses blowing.

They think
of rabbit ears and rabbit tails.
(And I do, too, I guess.)

Yes,
but not *just* now.
I think of rabbits running,
rabbits growing.

Yet, when the bells
start pealing in the steeple,
it is my habit
(since I'm a rabbit)
to think of *people*.

FELICE HOLMAN

11

THESE THREE

These three on Friday
Lay cloudy, dark and still:
    Shadows
        Of three crosses
            On cold Golgotha Hill.

These on Easter morning
Burst forth in bloom:
    Setting-egg.
        Tulip bulb.
            Good Lord's tomb.

                X. J. KENNEDY

THE SUN ON EASTER DAY

The way the sun on Easter Day
is dancing in the streets of sky
has put to shame the sluggard stay-
abeds who dull and dozing lie.

Get up! Get up! With harp and flute
make music fit to raise your roofs!
Grasses are leaping at the root.
Lambs are bounding on all four hoofs.

The very stones shake off their weight
and skip as seeds released from cold.
The soil itself, before too late,
blows up a storm of pollen gold.

All creatures, risen like the light,
in joyous motion join as one
to wish the winter gloom goodnight
and hail the dancing Easter sun.

NORMA FARBER

NOTE: An ancient legend claims that
the sun dances on Easter Day.

EASTER SONG

The Easter bells are ringing,
Loudly ringing,
"Jesus lives! He lives!"
The Easter bells are ringing
The song my heart is singing,
Softly singing.

BONNIE NIMS

SICILIAN EASTER SUNDAY

My neighbor always buys a lamb
for Easter butchering,
and ties it by his door,
and feeds it sweetest grass.
In the early mornings,
before I run down the river
to swim naked
and to let tadpoles slide
through my toes,
I plunge my hands into its deep wool.
Then, before Easter Sunday,
the lamb is seen no more.
And I think of the Easter Rebirth,
when Christ heals his wounds,
and I jump from the highest stairs
and roll His name
on the tip of my tight tongue
and fall and fall
and never get hurt,
while swallows circle
like black halos
over my head.

EMANUEL DI PASQUALE

15

THE EASTER BUNNY

There once was an egg that felt funny.
It was chocolate brown, and got runny
      When a clucky old hen
      Sat to hatch it, and when
She was done, what popped out was—a bunny!

Said the hen, looking down, "Well, I say!
You're a strange looking chick! But please stay
      Till you learn to say *peep*."
      "There's a date I must keep,"
Said the bunny, and hip-hopped away.

He did say, "Mrs. Hen, I thank you.
But I'm hatched now, and have work to do.
      Besides, it is best
      I get out of this nest,
For it's covered with chocolate goo."

He left then. And where did he go?
The fact is I really don't know.
      He might have come here.
      Look around you, my dear.
What's that on your bed?—Well, hello!

JOHN CIARDI

16

GRANDMA'S EASTER BONNET

Grandma's bonnet flutters to her head
each April
to be pinned in place by translucent fingers.
It has been sleeping,
silently sleeping in a round cardboard nest,
sleeping, sleeping in the darkest corner
of her closet.
Like a robin that reappears each spring,
it returns to its proper perch,
quietly preening in the soft sunshine,
ready for Easter Sunday.

BOBBI KATZ

AN EASTER PRESENT

Diamonds of brittle sugar
Circle the porthole
Of the ancient Easter egg I
Found packed away back
In our attic.

         "Why,"
Cries Mother, "that was mine!"

Taking turns we peer
Inside: on squirrels
(Just squiggly swirls
From a frosting gun), on the red roof
Of a rabbit house (white ears
Drooping from years
Of summers), on the river
Of glittering crystal candy that's begun
To run.

         Still,
The yellow dots of chicks, as if fresh-hatched,
Each with a grain of sugar in its bill,
Stand on a rock-hard green and grassy hill
They've not yet scratched.

"Aren't you glad," I ask,
"To find your egg again?
It's lasted all these Easters—it's
Come through!"

She nods a yes—
"I guess.

         But it's not mine.

Not any longer. Now
It's meant for you."

X. J. KENNEDY

WRITTEN ON AN EGG

Since Easter was a month ago,
Is this an Easter egg? Well, no—
Or—yes, why not? For who dares say
That hares do not lay eggs in May?
Scramble it, or boil, or fry it,
Any way you choose to try it.
May you get a great big lift
From my belated Easter gift,
On which I've scribbled, 'round the middle,
An up-to-now unanswered riddle
That silly fools and wise old sages
Have thought and fought about for ages:
Which came first? The egg? The hen?
I hereby solve it with my pen:
The egg, the egg! It was created
Hundreds of years before the hen—
Yes, but who could have laid it then?

The Easter bunny laid it!

EDUARD MÖRIKE
*translated from the German
by Doris Orgel*

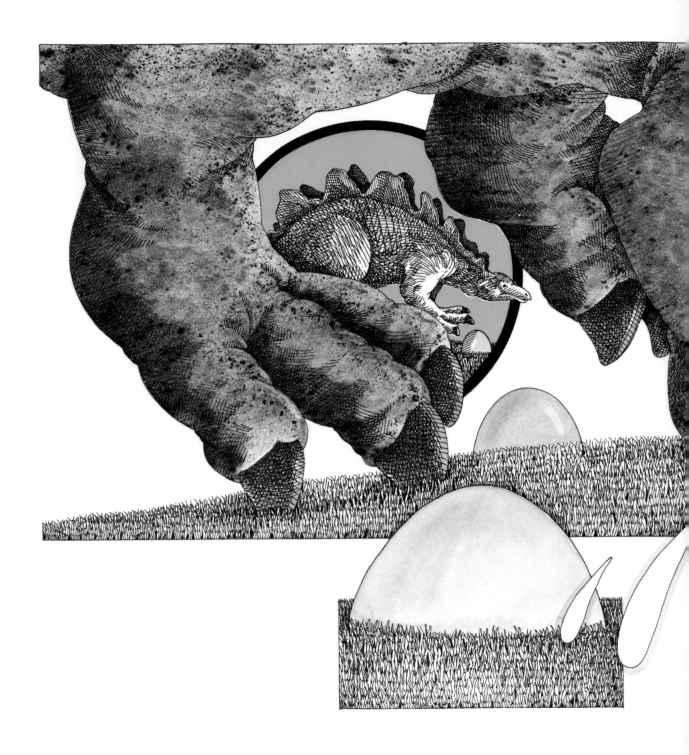

EASTER DISASTER

Higgledy-piggledy
Millions of years ago,
Dinosaurs walked on their
Tippy-toe paws

Hoping they'd find any
Easter eggs left by The
Dinosaur Bunny but
Couldn't because …!!

SCRONCH!

J. PATRICK LEWIS

THE EASTER PARADE

What shall I wear for the Easter Parade?
A dress that's the color of marmalade
With a border embroidered in light blue cornflowers
Like the edge of a meadow after spring showers
And a matching hat round as a top you can spin
And elastic to hold it on under my chin
And brand-new shoes whiter than newly-poured cream
With heart-shaped, golden buckles that gleam;
And I'll carry a small purse of butterfly blue
With a penny for me and a penny for you
To buy us both glasses of cold lemonade
When we walk, hand in hand, in the Easter Parade.

WILLIAM JAY SMITH

THE CHERRY-TREE CAROL

Joseph was an old man,
    And an old man was he,
And he married Mary,
    The Queen of Galilee.

Joseph and Mary walked
    Through an orchard good,
Where was cherries and berries,
    As red as any blood.

Joseph and Mary walked
    Through an orchard green,
Where was berries and cherries,
    As thick as might be seen.

O then bespoke Mary,
    So meek and so mild;
'Pluck me one cherry, Joseph,
    For I am with child.'

24

O then bespoke Joseph
    With words most unkind:
'Let him pluck thee a cherry
    That brought thee with child.'

O then bespoke the babe,
    Within his mother's womb:
'Bow down then the tallest tree,
    For my mother to have some.'

Then bowed down the highest tree
    Unto his mother's hand;
Then she cried: 'See, Joseph,
    I have cherries at command.'

O then bespake Joseph:
    'I have done Mary wrong;
But cheer up, my dearest,
    And be not cast down.'

Then Mary plucked a cherry,
    As red as the blood,
Then Mary went home
    With her heavy load.

Then Mary took her babe,
    And sat him on her knee,
Saying: 'My dear son, tell me
    What this world will be.'

'O I shall be as dead, mother,
    As the stones in the wall;
O the stones in the streets, mother,
    Shall mourn for me all.

'Upon Easter-day, mother,
    My uprising shall be;
O the sun and the moon, mother,
    Shall both rise with me.'

Traditional, English

EASTER UNDER THE WATER

Sea horses leaping and laughing
gallop on sands under kelp
while urchins, under the ledges,
are jiggling and scrambling to help.

       And the flounder lies flat.

It's Easter under the waters
and the starfish and garfish and prawn
are moving, each to his measure,
and dancing all night till the dawn.

       But the flounder lies flat.

Flipping in watery tumbles
sea creatures dance in their deep.
The skate and the squid, they are gliding
and the mussels are trying to creep.

       And the flounder opens an eye.

Hosanna to Jesus of oceans.
He is risen ages ago.
The fishes celebrate Easter
in jubilant pageant and show.

       Glory! the flounder is singing a hymn.

PETER NEUMEYER

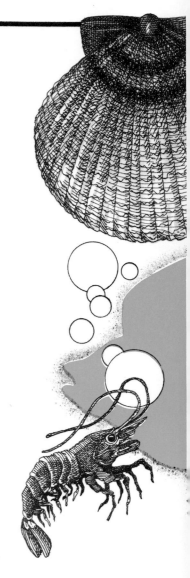

28

from EASTER MORNING

Is Easter just a day of hats,
Of Easter eggs from Bunny?
Is church on Easter something that's
Tomorrow if it's sunny?

You know the date: first Sunday—well?
"To follow the first full moon . . ."
"That follows the Vernal Equi————tell
Me!" . . . "nox!" That's pretty soon:

March 21. Oh, Easter means
The goddess of the spring
Who supervised the gardens, greens,
Birds, flowers, everything.

But Easter, oh, it means much more:
Christ risen from the dead;
His spirit in the heart before
We lose it in the head;

The resurrection of our love,
Compassion—sharing joy
In gratitude that we are of
This world: a girl, a boy.

DAVID MCCORD

KYRIE ELEISON

At Easter dawn
the men in Greece
fire off guns
as an act of peace:
CRASH BANG CRASH
in a roar of glee
as the sun comes dazzling
out of the sea
Kyrie Eleison
Ke tou chronou
The Lord is risen
and next year too . . .

Oh if we
could be given grace
to fire off our anger
into space
Missiles, rockets
into flight
aimed away
towards endless night

leaving the earth
clean, green, and bare
never a missile
anywhere

then we could shout
as we watched them climb
Kyrie Eleison
to the end of time

JOAN AIKEN

ACKNOWLEDGMENTS

Grateful acknowledgment is made to the following poets, whose work was specially commissioned for this book:

Joan Aiken for "Kyrie Eleison." Copyright © 1985 by Joan Aiken.

John Ciardi for "The Easter Bunny." Copyright © 1985 by John Ciardi.

Emanuel di Pasquale for "Sicilian Easter Sunday." Copyright © 1985 by Emanuel di Pasquale.

Norma Farber for "The Sun on Easter Day." Copyright © 1985 by the estate of Norma Farber.

Felice Holman for "Easter Habits." Copyright © 1985 by Felice Holman.

Bobbi Katz for "Grandma's Easter Bonnet." Copyright © 1985 by Bobbi Katz.

X. J. Kennedy for "These Three" and "An Easter Present." Copyright © 1985 by X. J. Kennedy.

J. Patrick Lewis for "Easter Disaster." Copyright © 1985 by J. Patrick Lewis.

Peter Neumeyer for "Easter Under the Water." Copyright © 1985 by Peter Neumeyer.

Bonnie Nims for "Easter Song." Copyright © 1985 by Bonnie Nims.

William Jay Smith for "The Easter Parade." Copyright © 1985 by William Jay Smith.

Zilpha Keatley Snyder for "Rabbits Are Nice Neighbors." Copyright © 1985 by Zilpha Keatley Snyder.

Grateful acknowledgment is also made for the following reprints:

Hilda Conkling for "Easter" from *Poems by a Little Girl.* Copyright 1920 by Stokes, copyright © 1949 by J. B. Lippincott Co. Reprinted by permission of Hilda Conkling.

Curtis Brown, Ltd. for "Written on an Egg" by Eduard Mörike, translated by Doris Orgel, from *Cricket, The Magazine for Children* 2 (1975) : No. 9. Copyright © 1975 by Open Court Publishing Co. Reprinted by permission of Curtis Brown, Ltd.

Little, Brown and Company for "Easter Morning"—#3 by David McCord from *One at a Time.* Copyright © 1974 by David McCord. Reprinted by permission of Little, Brown and Company.

Adam Yarmolinsky for "Little Catkins" by Alexander Blok, translated by Babette Deutsch. Copyright © 1966 from *Two Centuries of Russian Verse,* edited by Avvam Yarmolinsky, published by Random House, Inc. Reprinted by permission of Adam Yarmolinsky.